Bean's Big Day

WRITTEN BY **Karen Ackerman**   ILLUSTRATED BY **Paul Mombourquette**

Kids Can Press

News spreads fast as chicken pox in a town as small as Bean, Pennsylvania. So when old Mr. Trapp in the telegraph office got word that somebody from the moving pictures was coming, it didn't take long for everyone to find out.

Mr. Trapp always said the words out loud when he wrote down a message. Since the telegraph office was just a wooden door laid across two barrels in a corner of Mrs. Trapp's General Store, anyone nearby heard him.

That morning, I was eyeing Mrs. Trapp's jar of rock candy on a stick, trying to choose the biggest one for my penny.

But when I heard the news, I lit out for home without my candy *or* my penny.

"Some man from the moving pictures is coming to Bean, Daddy!" I yelled as I ran into the barn.

He looked up from milking but didn't say a word or miss a pull on the udders. Daddy was the calmest person I knew, next to Mama. But when I told him, "And he's looking to pick somebody to be *in* a picture show!" he let go of the cow.

"Whole town's set to go crazy then," he sighed. He put his head down and started milking again, but I could hear him laughing, real soft, under his hat.

"Go help your mama, Cricket," he told me.

My name is Eleanor, after Mama's best friend, but I get called
Cricket because on the night I was born, the crickets made the
biggest ruckus in all of Bean history.

Mama was hanging up wash in back of the house. When I told her
the news, she plucked the next pair of drawers from the clothes basket
and murmured "M'hm." Mama never got worked up, no matter if
something made her happy or sad.

I ended up hanging wash, too, and wishing
I had the stick of candy I'd left
Mrs. Trapp holding.

The folks in Bean took the news like Mama did. Bean was an "m'hm" kind of place.

The next day, Mayor John Allen called for a town meeting at the livery, which he did when anything happened, or was about to, in Bean. I supposed it would be as "m'hm" as everything else.

Slip, the livery boy, sang softly to himself and mucked out the horse stalls like always, while everyone else settled down for the meeting. Slip kept mostly to himself, and no one paid him any mind. He'd once been kicked by Mrs. Evers' gelding, which left him with a long half-moon scar on one cheek, and he seemed to turn even more quiet after that.

Children had to stay up in the loft. I sat between my two best friends, Lisabeth and Leeanna Comfry, who were look-alike twins and a year older than me. We spread out in the hay and dangled our legs. They jabbered about the picture show they'd seen with their grandma in Philadelphia.

Things got going when Mayor John Allen gave the tack table a few whacks with his hammer and bellowed, "This town meeting is called to order!"

Mrs. Morton, who was head of the Bean Ladies' Beneficent Society, stood up before the mayor had even finished hammering.

"*Decent* people know the moving pictures are the Devil's work!" she sputtered, tapping at her upper lip with a quivering hankie.

There were some "M'hms" from the crowd.

"Aw, Martha," Mr. Morton groaned, and he tugged her skirt in hopes she'd sit down. "Being in a picture show might be jim-dandy!"

The two of them started to spat, and then nearly everyone got to arguing over whether being in a picture show was something a decent person would do.

Mayor John Allen smacked down his hammer, but that didn't stop anybody.

The longer folks bickered, the more their tempers got as hot as Daddy's field boots in July. Suddenly, pocketbooks swung and hats swatted, a shoe knocked over Mayor John Allen's inkwell, and someone's threadbare sock got caught on the rafters.

I'd never seen the folks in Bean so worked up. Lisabeth and Leeanna laughed and said it was *just like the pictures!*

I didn't know exactly what the twins meant. I sure wanted to *see* a picture show. But if throwing things at folks was part of being *in* one, I didn't want to be picked.

Then Daddy hollered to me, "We're going home!" so I scrambled down the ladder. The three of us set off in the buggy. When I giggled over how Mrs. Morton had thrown her shoe at Mr. Morton, they hushed me with stern looks. I kept mum the rest of the way home.

The next few days were stormy for Bean. Mama and Daddy were out of sorts after the uproar at the livery. In town, ladies who'd been close as-nine-is-to-ten didn't even trade how-do's on the street, and I had to steer past fellas at fisticuffs outside Mrs. Trapp's store. The twins moped because they wanted to try being picked, but the Comfrys wouldn't allow it.

Daddy had been right, far as I could tell, because the whole town *was* acting crazy. The only one I saw going about his business as usual was Slip.

Bean's big day finally dawned. When I went downstairs to breakfast, Mama turned to me from the dry sink. "How do I look, Cricket?" she asked, and she did a spin around in a white lace dress that I'd never seen before.

You could've knocked me down with a feather, I was so stupefied.

"You're pretty as a *picture,* Amelia," Daddy chuckled.

"Daddy, you've got your good suit on!" I gasped as I sat down. There was even a wildflower pinned to his jacket.

"Yup!" he said with a grin, while Mama floated around the kitchen without hearing a word.

I suspected they'd woken up that morning under some kind of magic spell, and I felt a quick pinch of worry.

We skipped afternoon chores, piled into the buggy, and rode to town. Folks were already standing around waiting. Lisabeth and Leeanna waved to me from across the road, dressed in matching smocks and shoes dabbed with whitewash. I figured the Comfrys had changed their minds.

The clash at the town meeting seemed all but forgot. Just about everyone was wearing their Sunday best. I hardly recognized folks in their ruffles, bows and face paint! Some of them looked downright silly to *me*.

When I spied Mrs. Morton herself in the biggest flowered hat I'd ever seen, I knew that no one in Bean — not even my own mama! — was calling to mind a single "m'hm" they'd said. I was sure they'd *all* come under a magic spell.

It was late in summer and hot as tar and feathers. Everybody was edgy. Mayor John Allen tugged at his starched collar and studied his welcome speech. Several ladies began to wilt, having put on corsets to help them get picked.

The only sounds were of folks fidgeting and of Slip, who was leaning against the livery door, singing softly to himself. He had a pretty, church-choir kind of voice, and it gave me a shivery feeling. Though he was always singing, I'd never really listened before.

The ground trembled, and then we saw dust clouds flying up from the wheels of a roadster speeding down the only route that led into Bean. I heard the rustle of folks smoothing their finery.

When the roadster stopped in front of the livery, Mayor John Allen gave a little cough and commenced to make his speech.

One door opened, and the picture show man stepped out. He wore a fancy suit of clothes and a big homburg. The mayor carried on with his speech while the man strolled up and down the center of town, giving us a long, hard look.

I'd never seen such good posture or as many hopeful faces on plain Bean folks before. And Mama's face was the most hopeful of them all.

After sizing up the crowd, the picture show man turned back toward the livery. He strode over to where Slip still leaned against the door, singing.

The picture show man scratched his chin, cocked his head, and studied Slip up and down and side to side.

With a shy smile, Slip went on with his song.

Suddenly, the picture show man reached out, friendly-like, and slapped him on the shoulder.

"You'll be the first *singing* cowboy, son!" he gushed.

He led Slip toward the roadster, shuffled him inside, and climbed in after him.

We all watched wide-eyed as the picture show man, along with our crooning livery boy, sped out of Bean.

Mayor John Allen raised his arm to wave, but the rest of us — young and old — were struck dumb as doorposts.

Like chicken pox, the gloom spread fast. Folks drifted home, looking disappointed and with nary a word to each other. Everybody needed time to muddle through the shock of Slip being picked.

Daddy took my hand and led me to where Mama still stared down the road in disbelief.

"Amelia," he said softly, and when she turned to us, I was given a start by how worked up she really was.

Daddy let go of my hand and put his arms around Mama. "You're still pretty as a picture to *me*," he cooed.

He picked Mama up and swung her in a circle, sending the white lace dress sailing around her ankles. She let out a giggle. The more Daddy twirled her, the more Mama laughed.

But it was the same way I laughed when I skinned my knee, which was mostly to keep from crying.

Neither Mama nor Daddy said another word about it on the way home. Instead, they remarked on the new calf and how the barn needed painting before winter. And after supper, they settled into their parlor chairs like always. I went upstairs to my room.

At bedtime, Daddy came to tuck in my covers. He sat down and looked me in the eyes, ready to talk.

"Well, I guess we got our comeuppance today for acting like fools," he began with a hangdog look.

"Is Mama alright?" I asked in a whisper. I knew she was awful let down.

"Now, don't you worry," he soothed. "She'll be *fine*."

"Why did that man pick Slip for the picture show, Daddy?" I asked. "He's not one bit handsome!"

"I suppose he saw something special in Slip that the rest of us couldn't see," Daddy explained. "Or wouldn't see."

I thought that over for a minute. "Maybe we all need a good pair of spectacles," I suggested.

Daddy nodded and said, "Maybe so." Suddenly, he began to laugh, though I wasn't sure why. But he got *me* laughing, too. Then Daddy hugged me and turned off the lamp. I did a lot of pondering after he left.

A movie house opened in Bean the week before Christmas. The first picture show to play was *Song of the Old West,* starring "Slip the Singing Cowboy." When the lights dimmed and the show began, there wasn't one empty seat. Mama, Daddy and I sat right up front.

On the screen, Slip was bigger than life-size, and he looked handsome! His half-moon scar was gone. He wore spangled Western duds and rode a paint horse. He didn't look at *all* like the Slip we knew.

When the show was over, lots of folks began to clap and cheer for the boy they'd never paid any mind to.

"Not even a good pair of spectacles could've made them see that boy for who he is," Daddy said, shaking his head as we got up to leave.

Mama took my hand and sighed, "We were hardly willing to ourselves, Ben."

That's when I understood why none of us had seen what was special in Slip all along.

Maybe we just hadn't wanted to.

Because to see what's special in a person, I think you've got to be willing to pay them some mind.

At last, for Leslie;
always for Steven;
and with thanks to Larry Rosler – K.A.

For Molly Coppertop and Andy – P.M.

Text © 2004 Karen Ackerman
Illustrations © 2004 Paul Mombourquette

Kids Can Press acknowledges the financial support of the Government of Ontario, through the Ontario Media Development Corporation's Ontario Book Initiative; the Ontario Arts Council; the Canada Council for the Arts; and the Government of Canada, through the BPIDP, for our publishing activity.

Published in Canada by
Kids Can Press Ltd.
29 Birch Avenue
Toronto, ON M4V 1E2

Published in the U.S. by
Kids Can Press Ltd.
2250 Military Road
Tonawanda, NY 14150

www.kidscanpress.com

The artwork in this book was rendered in pen and ink with watercolor and white gouache.
The text is set in Adobe Garamond.

Edited by Debbie Rogosin
Designed by Marie Bartholomew
Printed in Hong Kong, China, by Book Art Inc., Toronto

This book is smyth sewn casebound.

CM 04 0 9 8 7 6 5 4 3 2 1

National Library of Canada Cataloguing in Publication Data

Ackerman, Karen, 1951–
        Bean's big day / written by Karen Ackerman ; illustrated by Paul Mombourquette.

ISBN 1-55337-444-4

I. Mombourquette, Paul II. Title.

PZ7.A1824Be 2004   j813'.54   C2003-903378-3

Kids Can Press is a *lorus*™ Entertainment company